PEEK-A-BOO YOU!

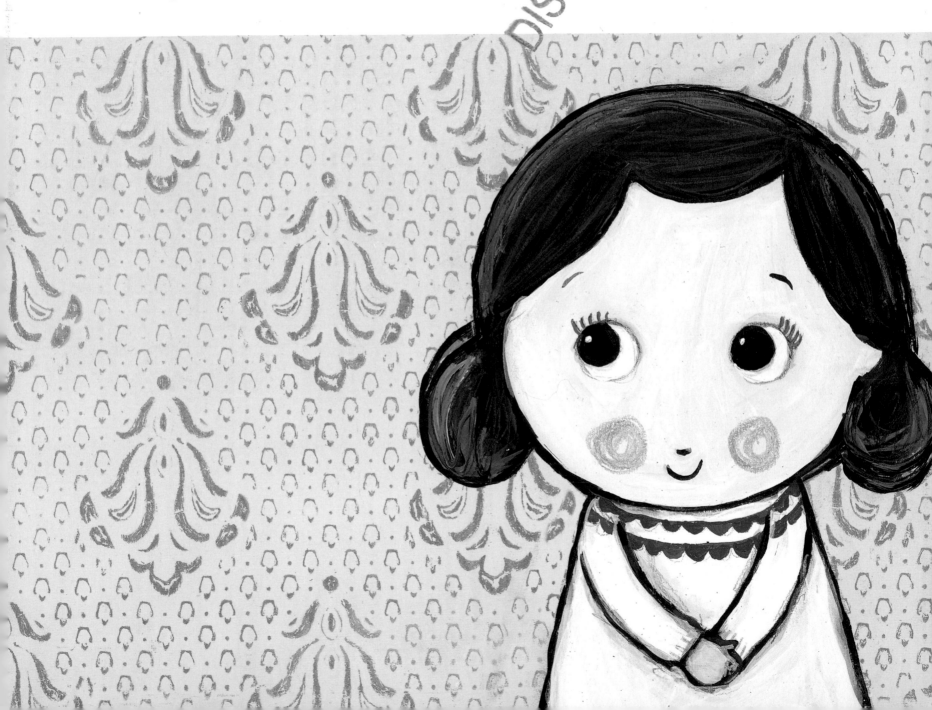

Peek-a-boo baby,
Peek-a-boo . . .

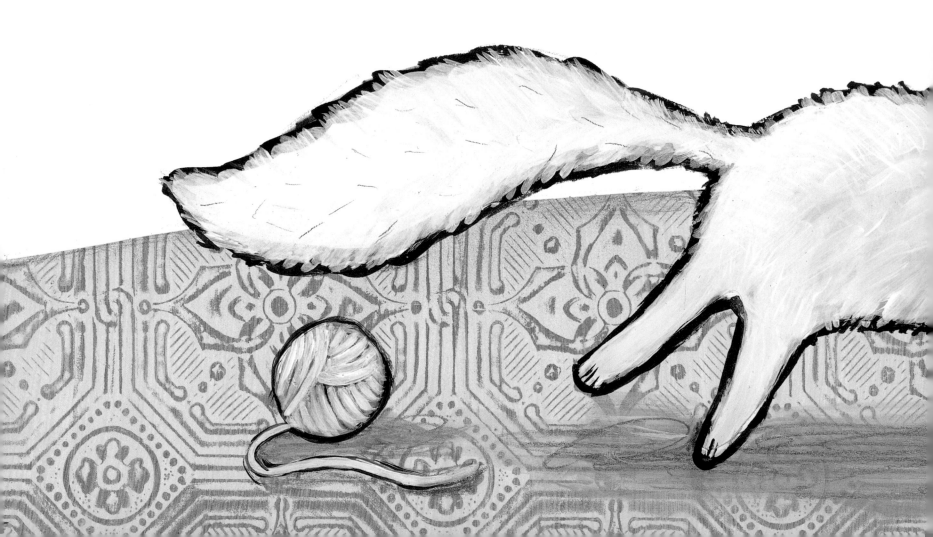

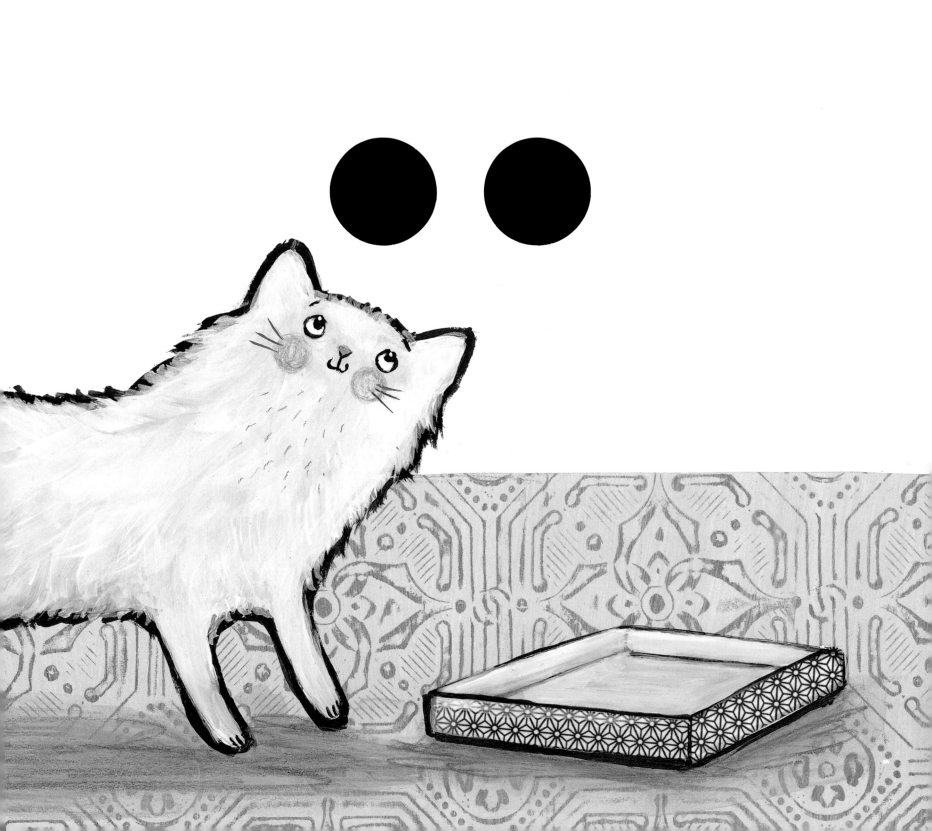

. . . shoe.

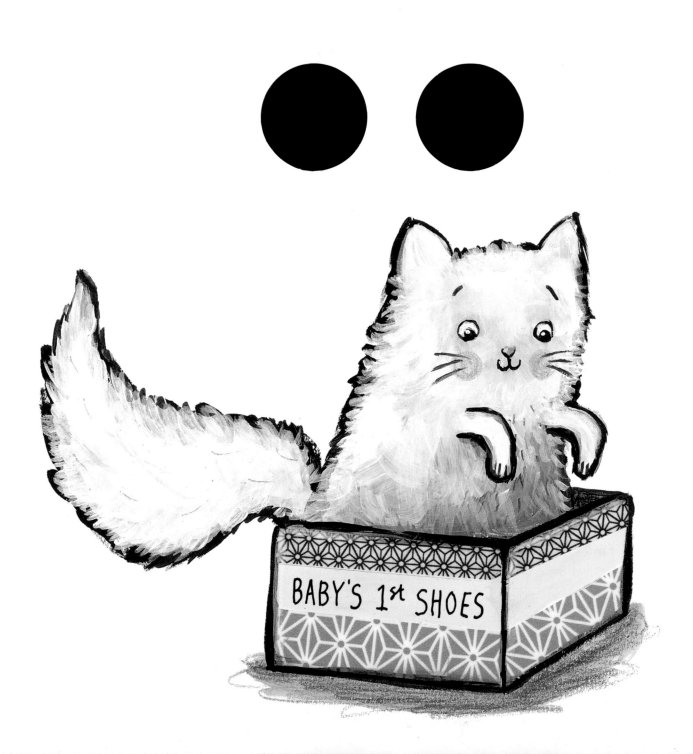

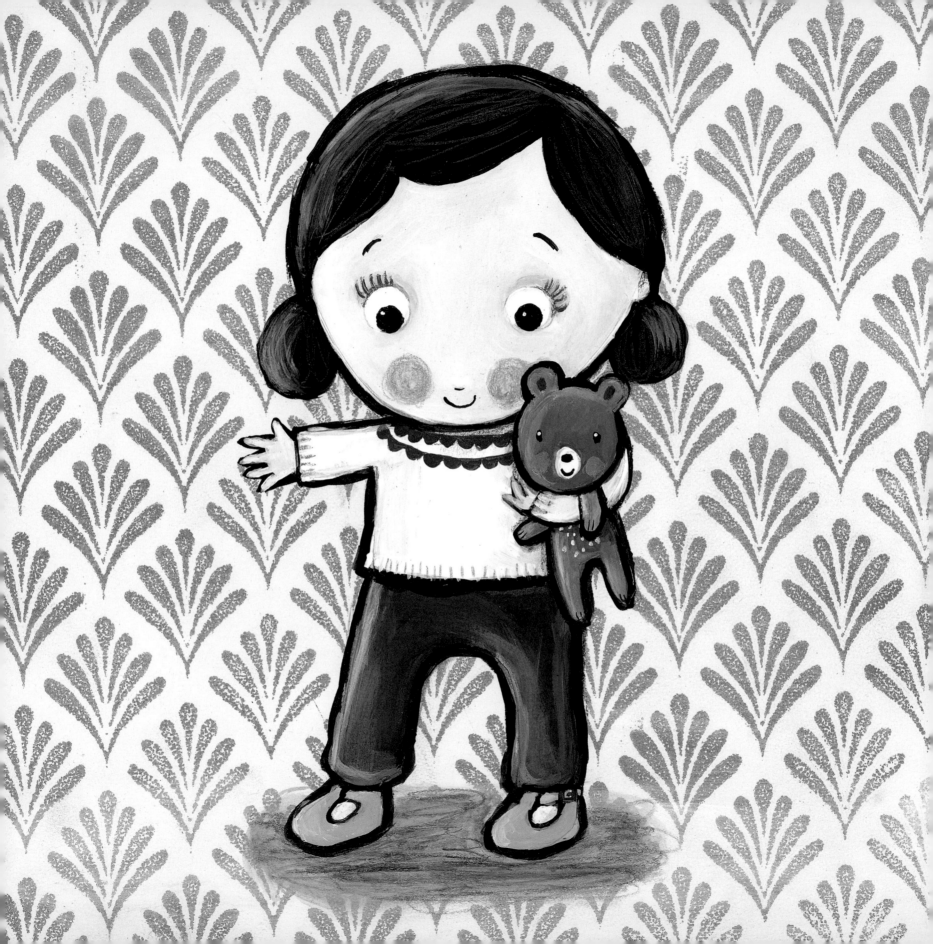

Peek-a-boo baby,
Peek-a-boo . . .

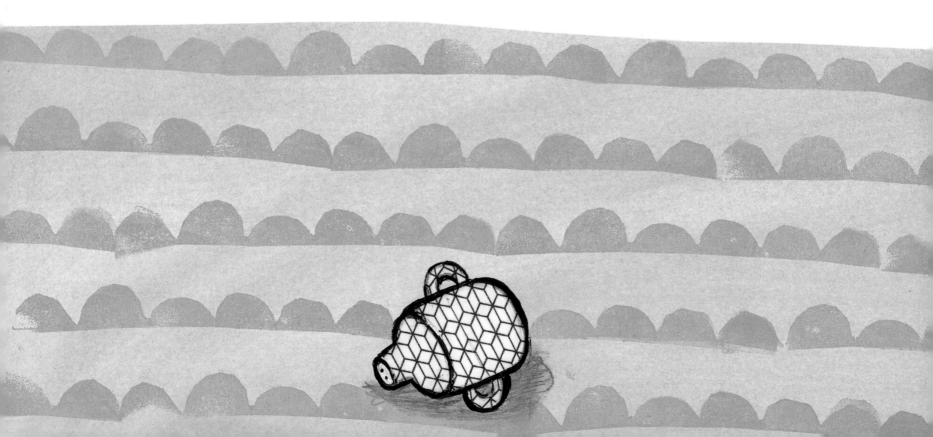

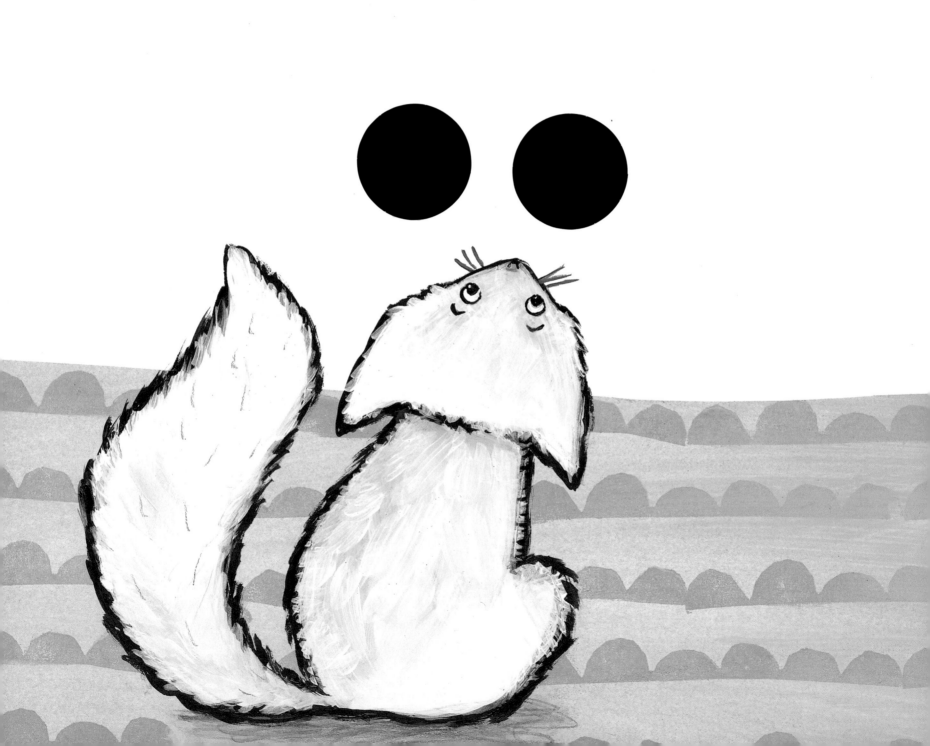

...chew.

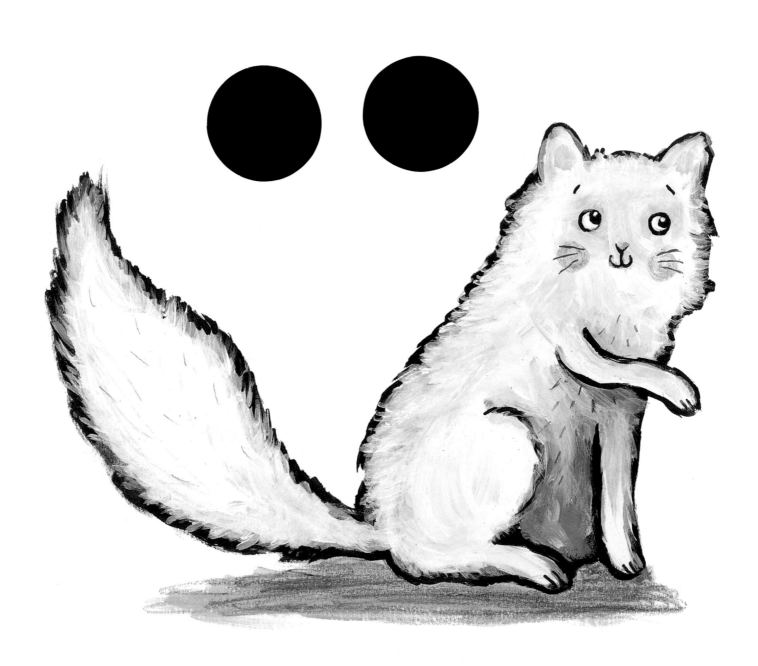

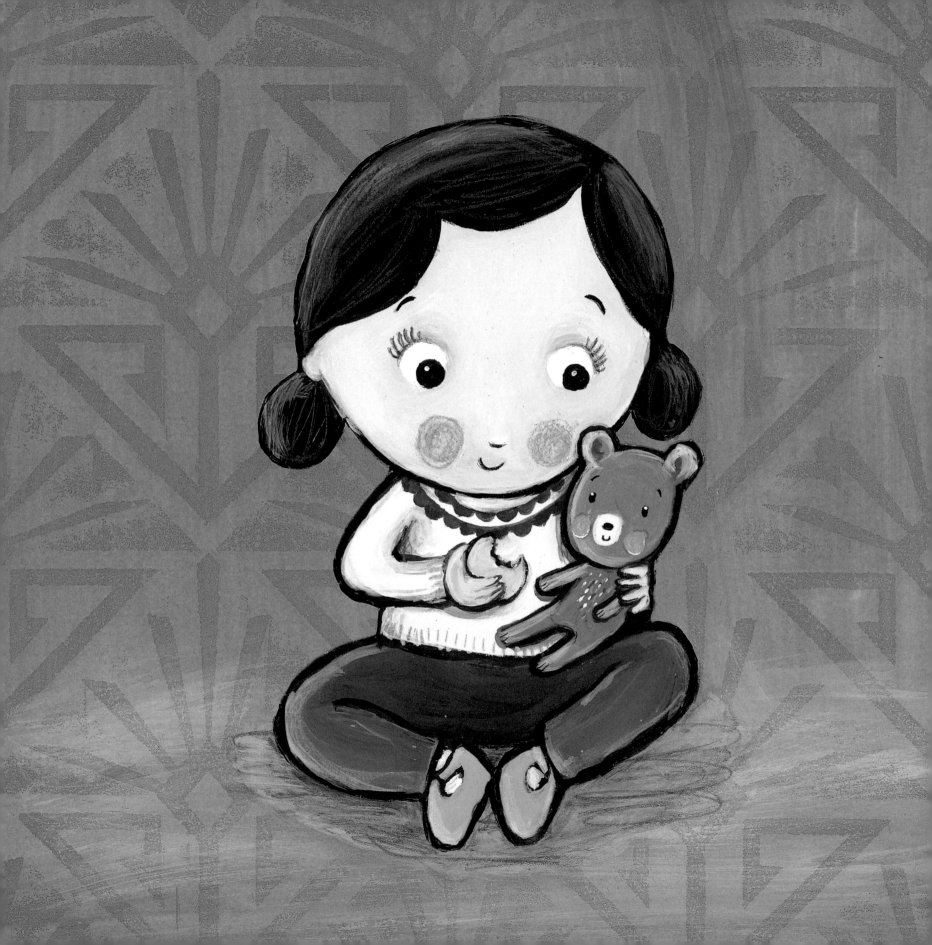

Peek-a-boo baby,
Peek-a-boo...

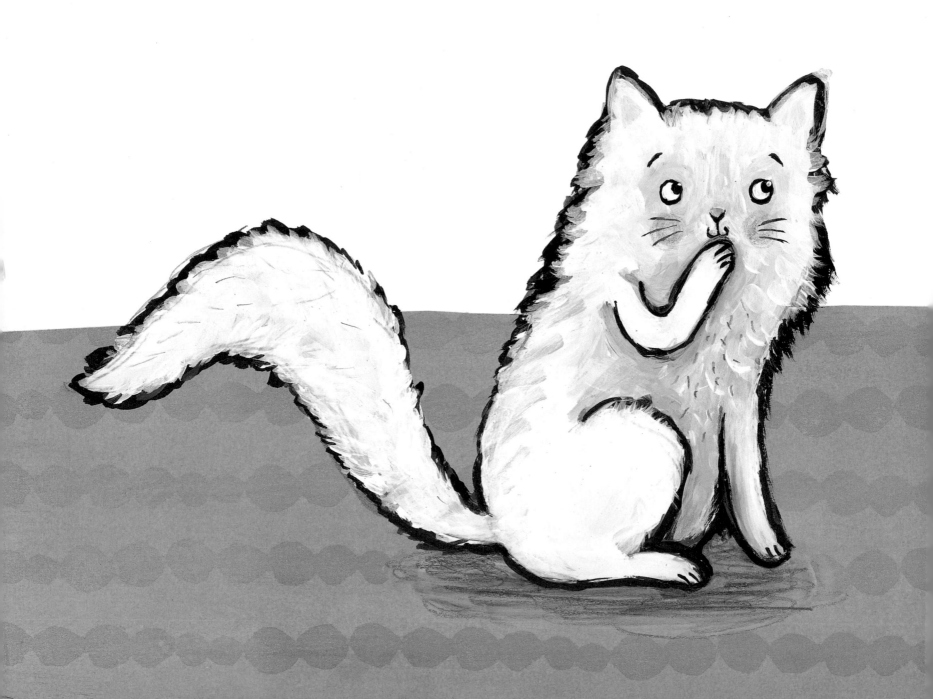

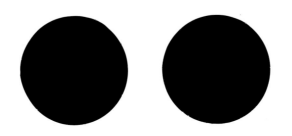
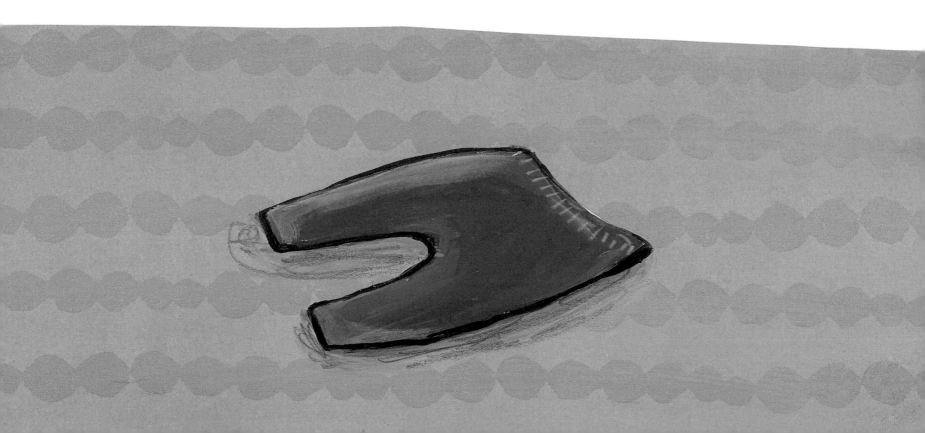

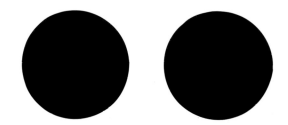

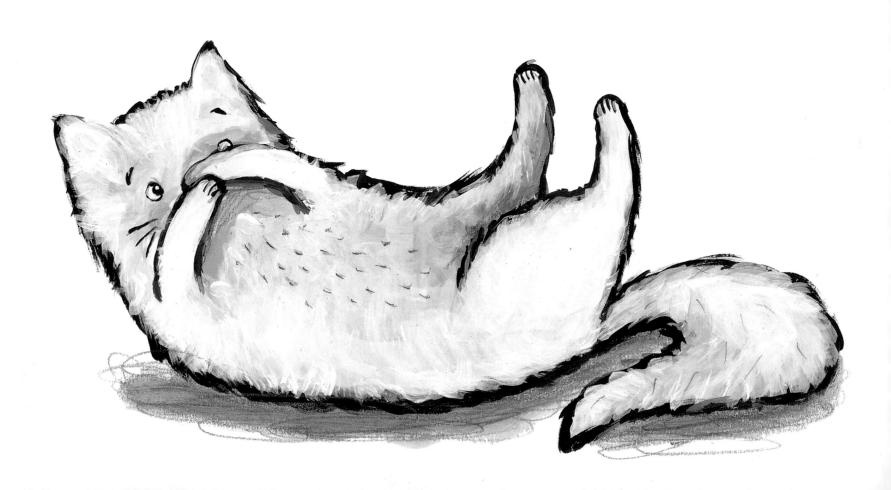

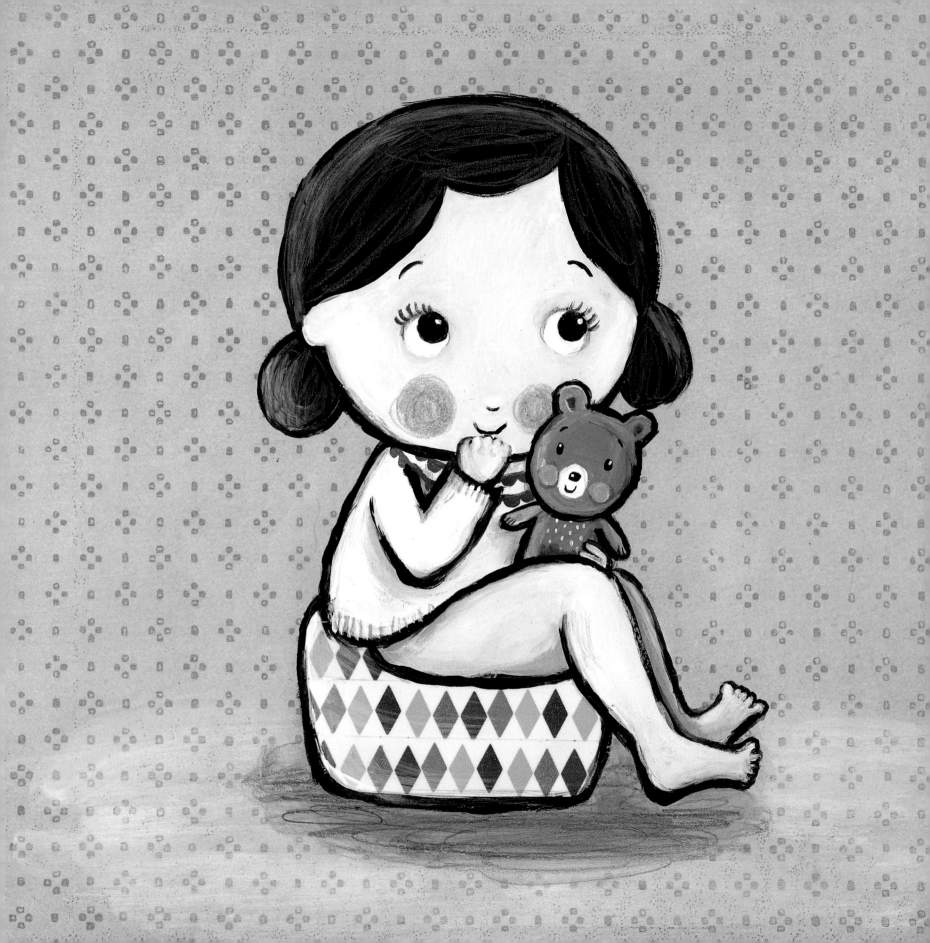

Peek-a-boo baby,
Peek-a-boo...

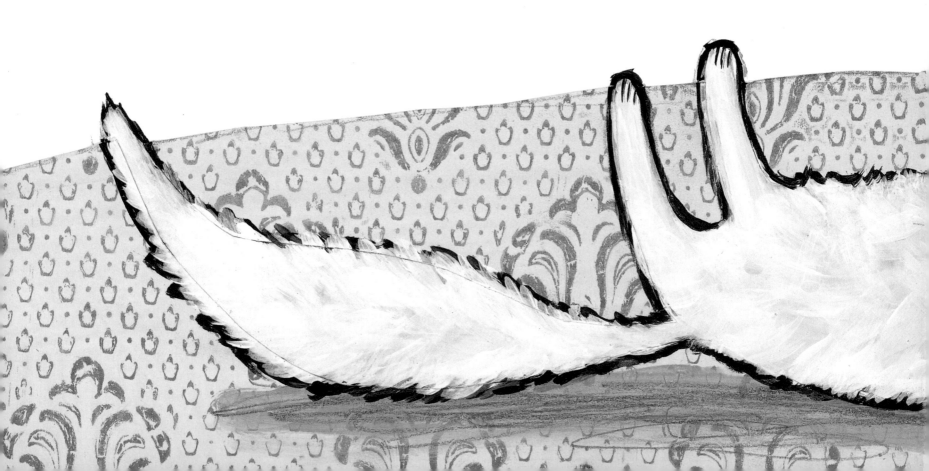

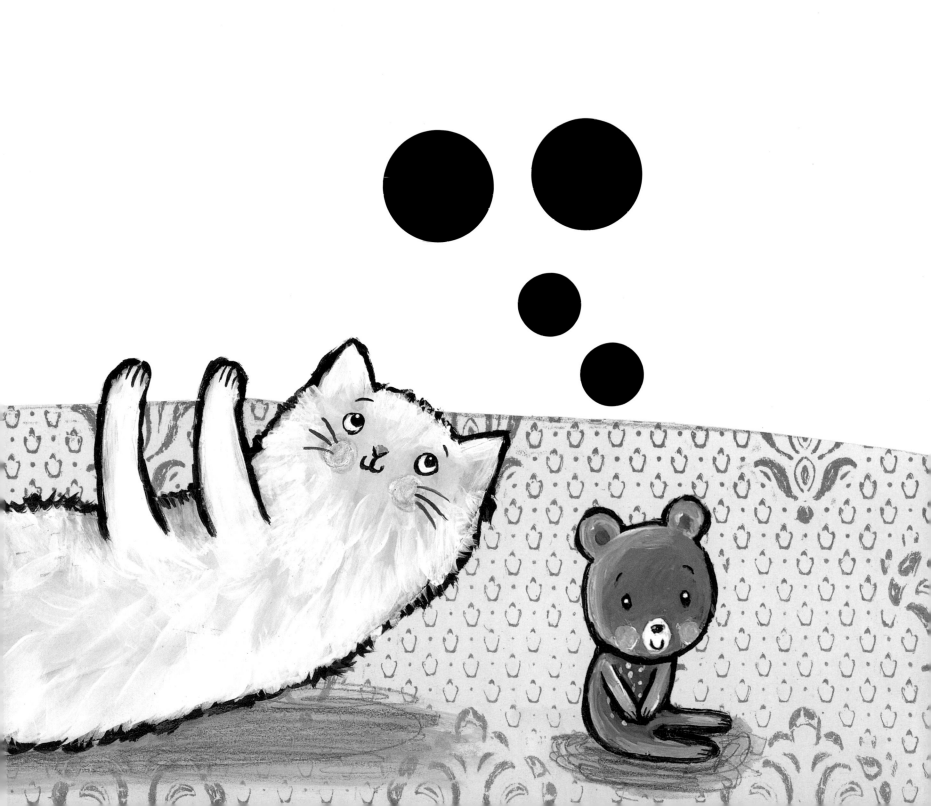

...new.

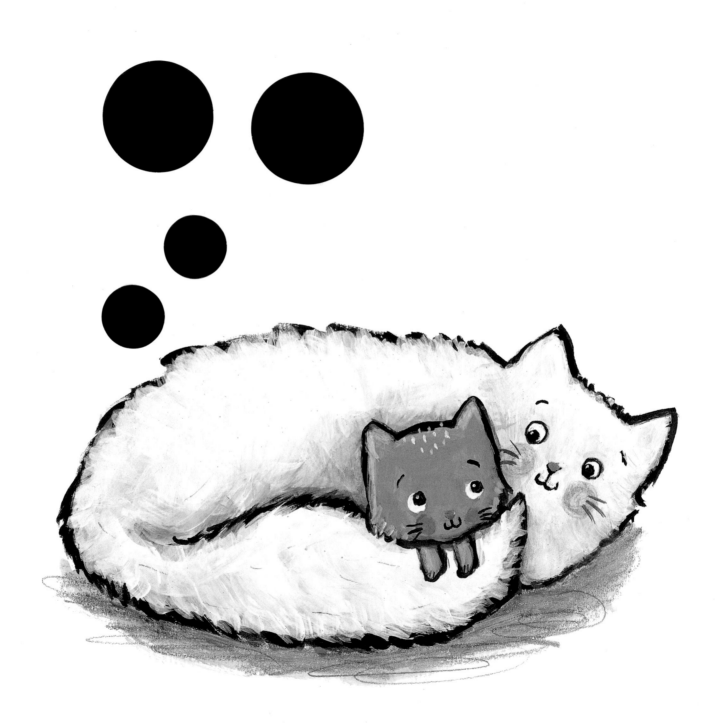

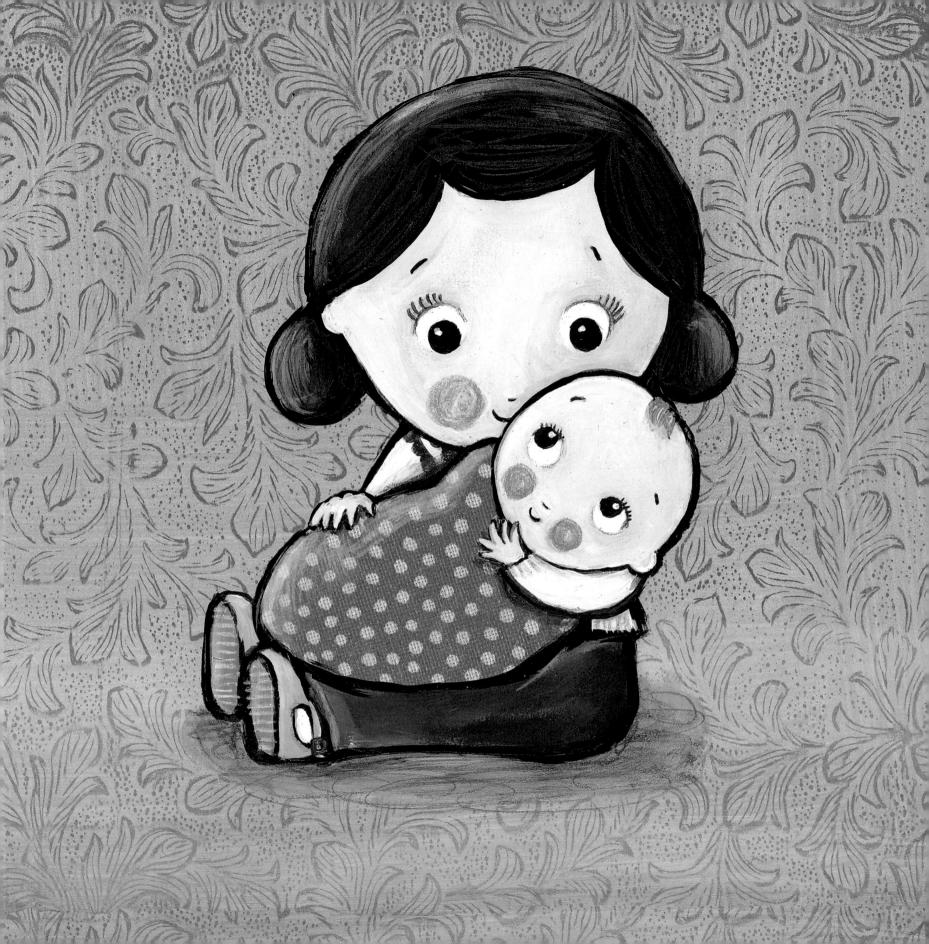

Peek-a-boo baby,
Peek-a-boo . . .

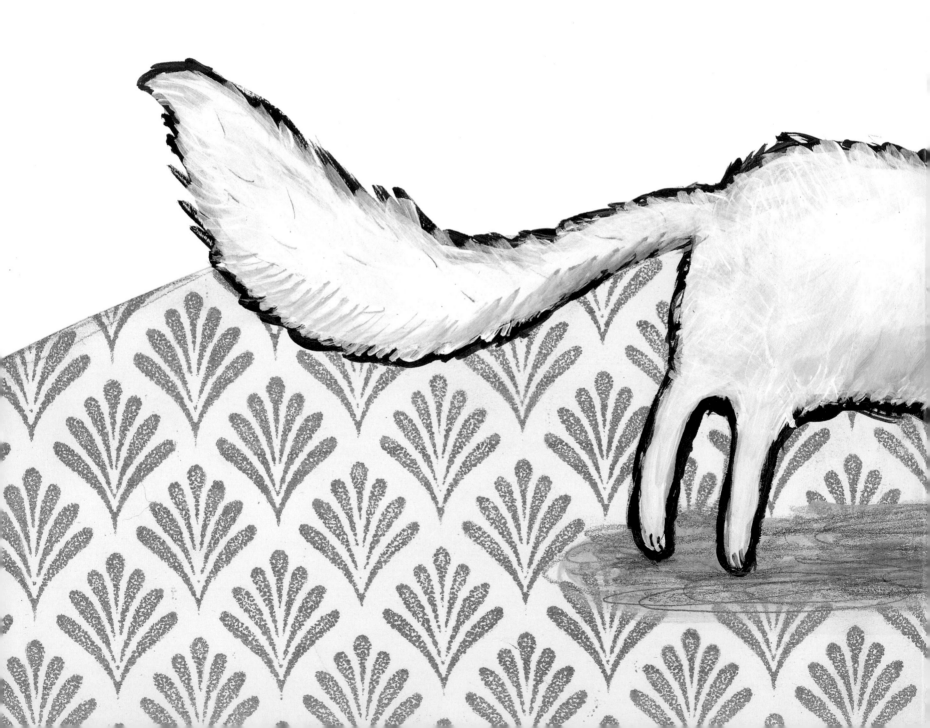

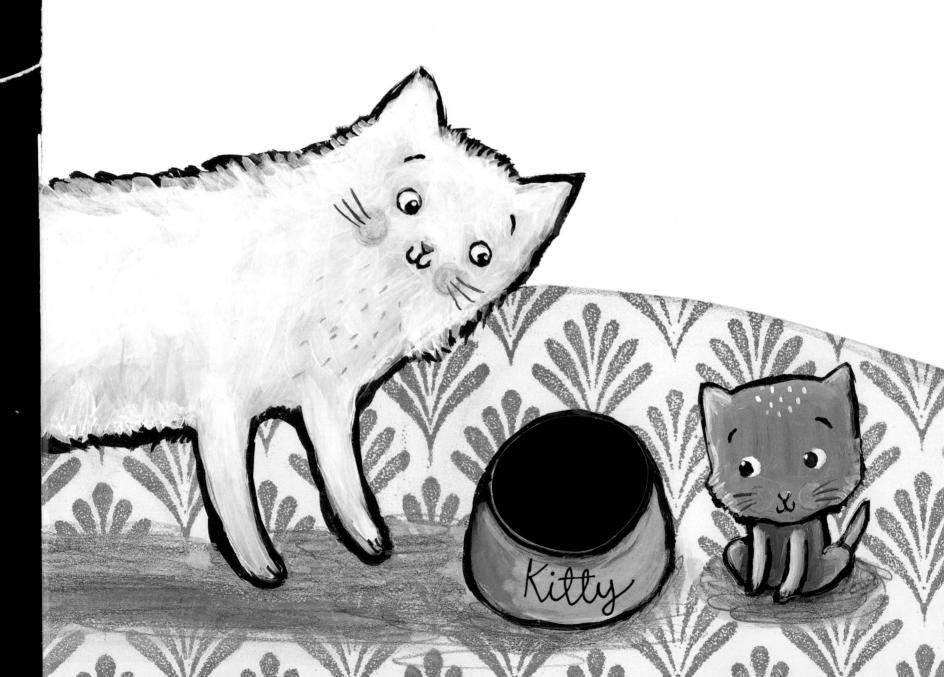

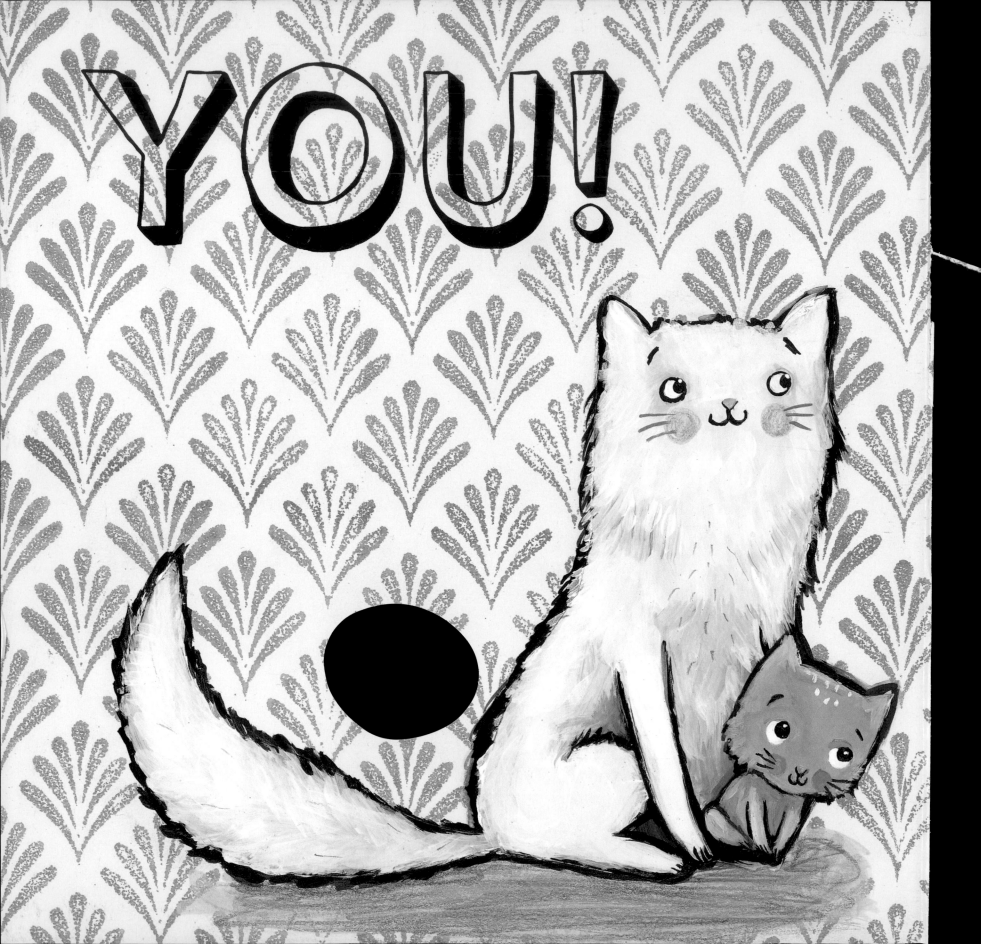